The Velveteen Rabbit

By Margery Williams

Illustrated by Christopher Santoro

Adapted from the original by Rose Reed

A GOLDEN BOOK · NEW YORK

Western Publishing Company, Inc., Racine, Wisconsin 53404

There was once a velveteen rabbit, and in the beginning he was really splendid. He was fat and bunchy, his coat was brown and white, and his ears were lined with pink sateen. On Christmas morning, when he sat wedged in the top of the Boy's stocking, with a sprig of holly between his paws, the effect was charming.

For at least two hours the Boy loved him, and then in the excitement of looking at all the new presents the Velveteen Rabbit was forgotten.

For a long time the Velveteen Rabbit lived in the toy cupboard in the nursery. He was naturally shy, and some of the more expensive toys snubbed him.

The mechanical toys were very superior and pretended they were real. The model boat caught the tone and referred to his rigging in technical terms. Even the jointed wooden lion put on airs. Only the Skin Horse was kind to the Velveteen Rabbit. The Skin Horse was very wise and had lived longer in the nursery than any of the others.

"What is REAL?" the Rabbit asked the Skin Horse one day. "Does it mean having things that buzz inside you and a stick-out handle?"

"Real isn't how you are made," said the Skin Horse. "It's a thing that happens to you. When a child loves you for a long, long time, then you become Real. By the time you are Real, most of your hair has been loved off, and you get very shabby."

"I suppose *you* are Real?" asked the Rabbit.

"The Boy's uncle made me Real many years ago," said the Skin Horse. "Once you are Real you can't become unreal again. It lasts for always."

The Rabbit sighed. He thought it would be a long time before this magic called Real happened to him.

One evening, when the Boy was going to bed, he couldn't find the china dog that always slept with him.

"Here," said Nana, who ruled the nursery, "take your old Bunny! He'll do to sleep with you!"

That night, and for many nights after, the Velveteen Rabbit slept in the Boy's bed.

At first the Rabbit found it rather uncomfortable. Then he grew to like it, for the Boy made nice tunnels for him under the bedclothes that he said were like the burrows the real rabbits lived in. And when the Boy dropped off to sleep, the Rabbit would snuggle down under the Boy's warm little chin and dream.

And so time went on. The little Rabbit was so happy that
he never noticed how his beautiful velveteen fur was getting
shabbier, and his tail coming unsewn, and all the pink rubbed
off his nose where the Boy had kissed him.

When Spring came, the Rabbit had rides in the wheelbarrow,
picnics on the grass, and fairy huts built just for him under the
raspberry canes.

And once when the Boy was called away suddenly, and the
Rabbit was left out on the lawn until long after dusk, Nana had
to go and look for him because the Boy couldn't sleep unless he
was there.

"Fancy all that fuss for a toy!" said Nana.

The Boy sat up in bed. "He isn't a toy," he said. "He's
REAL!"

When the little Rabbit heard that, he was happy, for he knew
that what the Skin Horse had said was true at last. He was a toy
no longer. He was Real. The Boy himself had said it.

One summer evening the Rabbit saw two strange beings
creep out of the wood. They were rabbits like himself,
but quite furry and brand new. They must have been very well
made, for their seams didn't show, and they changed shape
when they moved.

They stared at him, and the little Rabbit stared back. And all the time their noses twitched.

"Why don't you get up and play with us?" one of them asked.

"I don't feel like it," said the Velveteen Rabbit.

"Can you hop on your hind legs?" asked the other furry rabbit.

"I don't want to," answered the Velveteen Rabbit again.
One of the rabbits came up very close and sniffed.
"He hasn't got any hind legs!" the furry rabbit called out.
"And he doesn't smell right! He isn't a rabbit at all! He isn't real!"

"I *am* Real!" said the Little Rabbit. "The Boy said so!" And he
nearly began to cry. Just then there was a sound of footsteps,
and the Boy ran past the furry rabbits. With a stamp of feet and
a flash of white tails the two strange rabbits disappeared.

For a long time the little Rabbit lay very still. Presently the
sun sank lower, and the Boy came and carried him home.

Then one day the Boy grew ill. His face grew flushed, he talked in his sleep, and his little body was so hot that it burned the Rabbit when he held him close.

It was a long weary time, for the Boy was too ill to play. But the little Rabbit snuggled down patiently, and looked forward to the time when they would play in the garden and the wood like they used to.

Presently the fever turned and the Boy got better. The doctor ordered that all the books and toys that the Boy had played with must be burned. So the little Rabbit was put into a sack and carried out to the garden. Nearby he could see the raspberry canes that he had played in with the Boy. He thought of the Skin Horse and all that he had been told by him. Of what use was it to be loved and become Real if it all ended like this? And a tear, a real tear, trickled down his little shabby velvet nose and fell to the ground.

And then a strange thing happened. For where the tear had
fallen a flower grew out of the ground. And out of the flower
stepped a fairy. She came close to the little Rabbit and gathered
him up in her arms and kissed him on his velveteen nose.

"Little Rabbit, don't you know who I am?" she asked. The
Rabbit looked up at her, and it seemed to him that he had seen
her face before, but he couldn't think of where.

"I am the nursery magic Fairy," she said. "I take care of all the playthings that the children have loved. When they are old and worn and the children don't need them anymore, I come and take them away with me and turn them into Real."

"Wasn't I Real before?" asked the little Rabbit.

"You were Real to the Boy," the Fairy said, "because he loved you. Now you shall be Real to everyone."

And she held the little Rabbit close in her arms and flew with him into the wood. And she kissed the little Rabbit again and put him down on the grass.

"Run and play, little Rabbit!" she called.

But the little Rabbit sat quite still for a moment and never moved. He did not know that when the Fairy kissed him that last time, she had changed him altogether. He might have sat there a long time, if just then something hadn't tickled his nose, and he lifted his hind leg to scratch it.

And he found that he actually had hind legs! Instead of dingy velveteen he had brown fur, soft and shiny, and his ears twitched by themselves.

He gave one leap and the joy of using those hind legs was so great, he went springing about—jumping sideways and whirling round as the others did—and he grew so excited that when he did stop to look for the Fairy, she had gone.

He was a Real Rabbit at last, at home with the other rabbits.

Autumn passed and Winter, and in the Spring, the Boy went out to play in the wood. While he was playing, two rabbits crept out and peeped at him. One of them was golden brown all over, but the other had strange markings under his fur, as though long ago he had been stuffed.

The Boy thought to himself, "Why, he looks just like my old Bunny that was lost when I had scarlet fever!"

But he never knew that it really was his own Bunny, come back to look at the child who had first helped him to be Real.